BOSSY BEAR

DAVID HORVATH

Hyperion Books for Children
New York

To Sun-Min

Printed in Singapore
First Edition
10 9 8 7 6 5 4 3 2 1
Library of Congress Cataloging-in-Publication Data on file.
ISBN-13: 978-1-4231-0336-3
ISBN-10: 1-4231-0336-X
Reinforced binding
Visit www.hyperionbooksforchildren.com

Bossy Bear is very bossy.

He likes things his way all the time.

Bossy Bear spends his day telling others what to do.

CLEAN MY ROOM!

MAKE MY BED!!!

GIVE ME EVERYTHING!

HURRY UP!

WHAT DO YOU MEAN, DON'T WALK?!

THE DOLL...I WANT IT!
GIMME.

GIMME!

GIMME!

GIMME!

GIMME!

Hey, Bossy Bear...
do you want to play?

OKAY, IF WE ARE GOING TO PLAY, THEN WE PLAY MY WAY.

**No thanks,
you're too bossy.**

OH...

HELLO...?

Bossy Bear realized he was all alone.

Then, he met someone new.

"GIVE ME YOUR BALLOON!" said Bossy Bear.

**"You don't think I'm bossy?" asked Bossy Bear.
"You are bossy," said the turtle.**

"But you don't have to be."